Written In The Stars

Dazon Agenda, Volume 1

Aurelia Skye and Juno Wells

Published by Amourisa Press, 2016.

JOIN JUNO WELLS' NEW RELEASE LIST!

Click on this link (or copy and paste it into your browser):

http://eepurl.com/bnMJL5

Join Kit's Mailing List[1] (www.kittunstall.com/newsletter) to receive notification of new releases and access bonus chapters for your favorite books. You get six free books just for signing up. If you prefer to receive notifications for just one, or a few, of Kit's pen names, you'll have the option to select which lists to subscribe to at signup.

---

1. http://kittunstall.com/newsletter/

WRITTEN IN THE STARS (DAZON AGENDA, BOOK ONE)

3

Blurb

JADA WASHINGTON SUFFERS from a rare disease that has crippled her body and left her homebound. She copes by finding strength and support among the friends she's made on an online forum for those afflicted by the disease. When her friends start to go missing, she knows someone is taking them. Her investigation draws the attention of a handsome alien inquisitor sent by his home world to investigate the disappearances. As they unravel the reason for the abductions, she finds it almost impossible to disbelieve Ryland Breese's claim that she's his mate. She might not believe in soulmates, but she can't deny she's attracted to the sexy golden alien. One of his kind is stealing Earth women, but he's stealing her heart.

Chapter One

JESSMINDA42B9 WAS MISSING.

Jada had tried to be patient, but she was no longer clinging to the hope that her friend was busy doing something else. Like the other twelve women who had disappeared from the forum she ran, Jessminda had simply stopped posting.

At first, Jada hadn't realized there were disappearances. It wasn't completely uncommon for people to stop posting, or to go long stretches of time in between, even for the close-knit Internet community that composed the forum for sufferers of Kaiser's Syndrome.

It wasn't until the fourth member had dropped out of contact that Jada noticed their members were slowly disappearing. She had phone numbers for some of the missing women, and she had tried to call them all as the weeks had passed. Since they were Internet friends, she didn't always have a way to reach them outside of email or the phone number for some, even though she was the administrator of the forum, but she had continued to send emails every few days that went unanswered.

It was completely unlike the women, most of whom had been her friends since she'd established the forum eight years ago. They had all joined within a few months of her setting up the website for Kaiser's Syndrome sufferers after receiving her own diagnosis. It had been one of the ways she had coped, and as her mobility had dwindled, and her confinement at home had expanded, the forum had become one of the most important parts of her life.

She was deeply alarmed that twelve of her friends had fallen out of contact within the last two months, but Jessminda was particularly upsetting, because they were close friends. They had discovered within a few months of starting to chat that they lived in the same city, so whenever practical, they got together in person. With both of them confined to a wheelchair, it didn't happen as frequently as either would have liked, but it was typical for them to see each other at least once a month.

She hadn't heard from Jessminda for five days now, including emails and phone calls. She had called Jessminda's brother, who often stopped to check in on her, and when he had finally called her back less than thirty minutes ago, it had been with the disquieting news that his sister wasn't home. She usually informed him if she was going somewhere, just to be on the safe side.

Pradheep had also told her the neighbors hadn't seen Jessminda come or go in the last few days. Even in a wheelchair, her friend was a dynamo, often wheeling around the apartment complex or sitting out by the pool in the summertime. It wasn't like her to stay locked up in her apartment for days on end. She wasn't like Jada.

She'd tried notifying the police, but they had dismissed her concerns, taking the view she couldn't possibly be concerned about people not checking in on an online forum. The detective she had spoken with had been slightly rude about the whole thing, as though he considered her a waste of his time.

That meant she'd find no help with the authorities, so the only tool at her disposal was to slip into the underbelly of the world wide web and see what she could dig up. She made herself comfortable, slipped on compression gloves to protect her fragile wrists and finger joints, and began to finesse her way inside databases that were encrypted and technically supposed to be closed to her.

As she made her way around, starting with Internet providers and working outward after learning the identity of each woman who had gone missing over the past two months, she was temporarily amused at her own skills and familiarity with this side of life. Before she had gotten sick and received the unexpected diagnosis of Kaiser's Syndrome, she'd barely used a computer at all, except for work. She'd known how to copy and paste and create new documents, but had no knowledge of how the processes worked or the code that kept everything flowing.

Once she had displayed symptoms, they had moved quickly, and she'd been diagnosed with rapid progression less than a year after the first diagnosis. She had ended up in a wheelchair within two years, and it had changed her life. She stayed home most of the time now, and she had discovered she didn't mind it. The social creature she had been before was the one that felt like the façade that had finally fallen away, rather than her feeling like she was retreating into a shell and hiding from the world.

With all the free time on her hands, and looking for some way to use it, since she could no longer work as a paralegal at the busy law firm where she had been employed, she had learned all kinds of useful information. That had somehow led to her finding her way into hacking, almost by accident.

There was something fun and pleasing about solving the mysteries and breaking the code, and there was an illicit thrill that went with looking through all the deepest, darkest places of the Internet that had drawn her. She wasn't the best cracker around, but she was pretty good, and she had learned it all easily.

Two hours later, she leaned back in her wheelchair and pulled her hands from the keyboard, taking a break for a moment as she absorbed everything she had learned.

While it was still fresh in her mind, she put her hands back to the keyboard and pulled open her blog. It was an unusual posting for her, since she was far more likely to write about the daily challenges of living with Kaiser's Syndrome, or share her recipes and cooking, which was another hobby of hers.

She didn't touch on hacking or conspiracy theories even in a casual way usually, but her blog seemed like the best venue at the moment. The authorities wouldn't take her seriously, and she couldn't reveal her source of information to any recognized media establishment. She would have to act as a citizen journalist and hope enough people became interested in the topic to force the authorities to investigate.

This is a different blog post for me, everyone. As you know, if you're a reader of my blog, I've run a forum for Kaiser's Syndrome victims the last eight years. There are only about eighty-five members, so when they started to disappear, I took notice. These are the kind of women who don't just stop talking to us one day and drop off the face of the earth. For a lot of us, we're as close as family.

I called the local police, but Detective Thorne dismissed my concerns, so I had to become more creative. I've discovered it's not just my friends going missing. My source revealed there are almost four hundred active cases of missing women with Kaiser's Syndrome at the moment worldwide.

I assume you're not new to my blog, and you know what Kaiser's Syndrome is. Just to be on the safe side, let me give you a quick refresher course. Kaiser's Syndrome is a genetic condition caused by inheriting a tiny fragment of extra DNA on the ninth chromosome. It only causes symptoms in women and is passed from mother to daughter, but it's only active if the father is also a carrier.

It was only recently discovered, and doctors don't know everything about it. Dr. Hans Kaiser was the first to label and identify it. His patients who had it suffered from the same shared genetic anomalies, including an extremely rare blood type identified as AO-negative. That's due to the genetic mutation, and the link is still unexplained.

Also unexplained is why Kaiser's Syndrome affects mostly women of African or Indian descent. Eighty percent of women who have Kaiser's Syndrome are in those two nationalities. Men can receive the gene from their mother, but they're only ever carriers. There hasn't been nearly enough testing to determine why that is, or if it's more prevalent among other races of men, or also mostly confined to Indians and Africans.

So the question becomes, what happened to four hundred women with a disease that progressively affects their neurological and musculature system, rendering us disabled and virtually immobile as the disease progresses? Is there a connection? It's true that people go missing every day. According to the National Crime Information Center's website, there are more than six hundred thousand open missing persons cases right now.

Am I simply seeing a coincidence? Am I trying to generate a link where none exists? Or is there someone targeting women with Kaiser's Syndrome for some reason? I could think of a few theories as to why, and the most predominant one would be medical experimentation, but that makes little sense. I'm certain many of us would volunteer for experimentation if we could get the funding and the attention necessary to make Kaiser's Syndrome a known and easily recognizable disease with public urgency for a cure.

It's true pharmaceutical companies are motivated by profit, and they've certainly done underhanded or shady things in the past, but it seems beyond the norm even in that industry to actually kidnap people on whom to experiment. So what is the explanation?

I eagerly await any theories, and I encourage you to share this post. Only through public demand will authorities take action. Right now, disappearances are scattered over multiple jurisdictions worldwide, and I'm not even certain anyone has made the connection besides myself. Help me to change that, loyal readers.

After finishing the post, she sat back as a wave of exhaustion swept through her. She had certainly depleted all her energy today, and suddenly all she wanted to do was go to bed and sleep for a thousand years. Knowing it would be a while before anything started happening with the blog post, and assuming she was being wildly optimistic that any public official would act on the information contained therein anyway, she decided to have an early night.

Concern for her missing friends filled her mind, but it was no match for the pure physical exhaustion in her ravaged and withered body. She hated being at the mercy of the disease, which trapped her in a useless body and zapped all her energy. As she drifted off to sleep, she couldn't help indulging in a slight fantasy, one in which her friends and the other women with Kaiser's Syndrome were taken for a noble purpose, one that resulted in a cure for everyone. She wasn't normally so Pollyannaish, but on the edge of sleep, she indulged the optimistic thought until unconsciousness swept over her.

Chapter Two

IT HAD BEEN ALMOST a week since her blog post, and while Jada certainly hadn't forgotten about it, it had slipped to the back of her mind in a way. There had been somewhat of a flurry in the first few days, and it had received the most hits of any of her blog posts ever, along with countless retweets on Twitter and shares on Facebook, but all the excitement and buzz generated from the article had done nothing to interest the authorities.

Jada continued trying to contact her friends, and she grew more alarmed as two others stopped posting on the forum and didn't respond to their emails any longer. She didn't have phone numbers for those women, so she had no other way to contact them, but her concern grew.

On the forum, the women were discussing ways to protect themselves, and Jada wished she had a gun like some of the ladies. It had always seemed like an unnecessary device before, since she lived in an urban area with police that responded quickly, but now that they weren't responding at all, she was feeling weak and terrified, which pissed her off. She had fought long and hard for her independence, and she resented that whatever was happening could make her feel frightened to even open her door long enough to check her mail or arrange to take the bus to the market.

Acting from that apprehension, she was cautious that afternoon when her doorbell rang. It could be her latest delivery from Amazon or a neighbor. Perhaps it was even her stepsister, though that seemed unlikely since Erica was firmly immersed in her own world and only stopped by to visit her two or three times a year despite living within fifty miles.

Grasping the poker from the fireplace, she moved her electric chair to the door, peeking out through the peephole that had been lowered and modified so she could see it comfortably from her chair. A strange man stood on the other side. She couldn't see all of him, but he appeared a bit bland in his dark suit. "Who is it?" she asked through the door.

"Are you Jada Washington, author of *Jada's Blog*?"

Jada's stomach tightened with dread that she had no logical reason to feel. The unknown was scary enough, and suspecting she was being targeted—well, her and every other woman with Kaiser's Syndrome—was plenty of reason to be cautious and wary. "You didn't answer my question."

"My name is Ryland Breese, and I'm here to investigate the disappearances of the women you mentioned in your blog."

"Show me your badge."

He hesitated. "I don't have a badge," he said softly.

She shook her head, a harsh laugh escaping her. "Do you really think I'm going to let you in without a badge? I don't know who you are."

Without awaiting a reply, she backed away from the door before turning her chair to face it a few feet away. She was hoping he had gone away, but when he knocked again, she gritted her teeth.

"Please, Ms. Washington, I only want a few moments of your time."

"Or maybe you want to kidnap me and make me disappear like my friends. Go away now before I call the police."

There was silence, and it lengthened to the point where she was starting to feel optimistic that the person on the other side of the door had given up and chosen to go away. If he was really investigating the disappearances, he would produce a warrant or a badge before he got into her home. If he had other, more nefarious plans, at least she wouldn't make it easy on him by opening her door and inviting him in for sweet tea and abduction.

Just as she had taken a deep breath of relief, the door started to glow with a golden light that emanated under the door sill and around the cracks. She watched with openmouthed shock as the locks unlocked themselves, all unlocking in a neat and orderly fashion one after the other. As a final step, the chain fell out of the plate before dropping to the wall. She lifted her poker with abject terror as the door slowly opened, and the bland man stepped inside.

"What are you doing? Get out of my house."

He ignored her, pausing to close and lock her door again, doing so by placing a palm against the door. After she was locked in with him, he took a couple of steps toward her before pausing and holding up his hands. "Please, Jada, I mean you no harm."

"Who are you? Why are you here?"

He sighed, and then the air around him seemed to twitch and vibrate for a moment. It was like watching blurred pay-per-view at fast-forward. One second, he was the nondescript man, and the next, he was far taller, far more imposing, and anything but bland. His skin was brown, perhaps even a few shades lighter than her own, but with golden luminescence that was beautiful and hypnotic at the same time. He had tawny-brown eyes with that same gold shine to them, and his features were strong. While he wasn't classically handsome, he was certainly compelling to look at.

He'd also gotten taller and far broader in the shoulders, which emphasized his narrow waist and flat stomach. The dark suit had morphed into a simple black garment that covered him from neck to ankle.

She sagged in her electric wheelchair, shaking her head as she tried to deny what she was seeing; what she had just seen. "What's going on?"

He bowed his head slightly, and it appeared to be a gesture of respect. "As I said, I'm Ryland Breese of the Dazon Empire. I'm an inquisitor, which is akin to an earthling detective. Your blog post caught my attention. You have similar occurrences noted that match events occurring in an investigation by my home world. I've come to Earth to find the answer to where your friends have disappeared to."

She shook her head, gripping the poker even tighter between both hands. "I don't buy it. Why would some alien dude care about a bunch of missing Earth women?"

She wanted to say he arched a brow, but she realized he had no eyebrows. He just had a thick mane of golden brown hair that flowed from his forehead down to the back of his neck, though there was no hair on the sides of his head. She didn't know if that was a deliberate styling choice, or if perhaps they didn't grow hair there.

Or perhaps she was going crazy by believing this was actually an alien. It seemed far more likely it was someone pretending to be an alien, simply because that was what logic suggested. However, if this was a pretense, the person had certainly done a good job of presenting an alien appearance, and how had they managed that trick with her door?

"May I sit down, Jada?"

She almost snapped at him, wanting to demand to know when they had become familiar enough to be on a first-name basis, but if he really was an alien, it seemed like the kind of lapse in etiquette she should just let slide. Still clinging fiercely to her poker, she waved a hand toward the recliner in her living room. She had gotten rid of all the other furniture, because it impeded the path of her chair, and visitors were infrequent. "Have a seat, Mr. Alien."

"Ryland Breese," he said for the third time as he walked past her, nodding his head again in that same fashion that suggested it was a show of respect. He sat down on her lounger, and though it was cushiony and overstuffed, he looked far too big for it. It was like an adult trying to squeeze into a child's recliner.

Any urge she had to laugh faded when she met his golden-brown eyes again. There was genuine concern reflected there, and also what looked like...guilt? She wasn't certain. If he was an alien, could he even feel guilt? She wheeled herself a bit closer, but certainly not within easy grabbing range, and set the poker across the arms of her wheelchair in a decisive fashion, clasping the metal rod in both hands as she stared at him. "Explain to me why any aliens would care about earthlings?"

"May I share a little of the history of our empire with you?" At her nod, he said, "The Dazon Empire is slowly dying out. Three generations ago, we were at war with an enemy who unleashed a biological weapon upon us. We managed to defeat the enemy, but it was only as the war came to an end that we started to see the effects of the biological weapon.

"The primary effect it had was to render Dazon females sterile. Some women were still getting pregnant, but far fewer than we needed to keep our species alive."

She made a small sound of distress on behalf of the women, finding sympathy for them even if this was all some sort of elaborate hoax, or the women didn't even exist. She could empathize, having had to give up her dreams of motherhood upon realizing she had Kaiser's Syndrome.

She couldn't risk passing on the disease, and with rapid progression, she hadn't been in a proper state of health to get pregnant anyway, even if there had been a prospective father in the picture at that point. Her fiancé had been long gone, disappearing shortly after her diagnosis and before things even got really bad. Barry never would have made it through seeing her confined to a wheelchair and having to adapt to that kind of life.

"Our scientists have done what they can, and some genetic manipulation is possible, but now when there's a successful and healthy pregnancy, eighty percent of the time it results in a male child. We're not certain if that's a direct side effect of the biological weapon, and it was designed to work away, or if it's a result of the genetic manipulation our scientists use, and the fact that males seem to be immune to the effects of the biological weapon."

"So you have very few women who can get pregnant, and when they do, four out of five babies born are male?"

Ryland Breese nodded again. "Yes, that's exactly right."

She frowned at him. "It sounds like a terrible problem for your Empire, but I still don't see the connection with my missing friends."

He nodded. "For the past generation, we've been desperately searching for a genetic match among other species, hoping to find women who could bear Dazon young before we're completely extinct. It's been slow going, and politics hamper how to proceed should we find a compatible species. There is debate between simply snatching the women and forcing them to bear our young, or attempting to solicit their compliance with material things, or perhaps treaties and information exchanges with the governments of the planet involved."

"And have you reached a consensus?"

He hesitated for a moment before shaking his head. "The only resolution our General Council has fully embraced is the women must be compliant and consenting. We might be on the verge of extinction, but that doesn't justify kidnapping a race of sentient beings to save our own. We don't have a firm plan in mind, and there's an outspoken minority that protests this. The High Council has never given their official position, but it's well known they align with the minority."

Her head was starting to hurt. It was simply from the overload of information and trying to absorb the fact that maybe, just maybe, this guy was a legitimate alien and not some actor or hoax. "What... Do you think Earth women are compatible?"

Ryland shrugged. "I'm not certain. I'm not tasked with the scientific investigation into finding a compatible species. I know Earth women have been tested, but it's my understanding there was no clear outcome. However, the scientist in charge went on hiatus two months ago, as did a small number of his core team. I've been unable to find any trace of Jorvak Ha or the others. It's my supposition that perhaps Dr. Ha found a link between our species' genetics and a small subset of your species' genetics."

She let out a ragged exhale. "You're going on the assumption that women with Kaiser's Syndrome are genetically compatible with Dazon men?" The idea of being intimately...compatible with the golden alien squished into her recliner was distracting and threatened to derail her from the conversation as erotic images flickered through her mind. Forcing her attention back to him when he nodded, she asked, "And what was Jorvak Ha's position on how to handle finding a compatible species?"

His expression closed, and his lips tightened as he radiated evident anger. "Dr. Ha firmly believes we should take the women with or without their consent and use their genetic material as needed."

Her head spun, and she slumped even further in her chair. "Do you think my friends have been abducted by aliens?" She let out a laugh, but it held a slight edge of hysteria. "I want to say that sounds crazy, but it's actually the most logical theory I've heard or come up with myself since I started noticing their disappearances. Do you know where my friends are, and where the other women have been taken?"

"No, not yet, but I hope to figure that out with your assistance, Jada."

She blinked at him, shocked she was in this position. Was she really having a chat with some intergalactic detective-type who was investigating missing persons cases of galactic proportion? Were her friends really being held as some sort of breeders for a desperate race of aliens on the verge of extinction? It truly was no crazier than some of the other theories she had come up with or had been suggested on her blog. With a helpless shrug, she said, "I'll help however I can, but I'm not going to be very useful to you in this chair, Mr. Breese."

"Call me Ryland, Jada. And if you permit me to do so, I can solve that problem."

Chapter Three

SHE STARED AT HERSELF in the mirror in disbelief. It had taken some persuading on his part to convince her to accept an injection from an alien device, especially when he had explained it held nanobots. They would quickly adapt to her human genetics and restore her body to a state of perfect health. They wouldn't be able to remove Kaiser's Syndrome, because they couldn't reprogram her DNA or remove the fragment of the ninth chromosome that shouldn't be there, but they would keep her body in a healthy balance, and she would no longer be confined to the chair.

With that promise, she had been willing to try anything, and now, less than an hour later, she stood in front of her mirror and admired herself.

She'd always been on the curvy side, and the last eight years being ill, with six of those confined to a wheelchair, had added some extra pounds despite regular physical therapy. Now, she was in the best shape of her life, better than she'd ever been. She still had soft curves and a rounded tummy, but she could see the biceps flex under the skin when she moved her arms, and she could feel the rock hardness of her abs beneath the soft layer of flesh.

He knocked on the door, interrupting her visual inspection of her changed body, calling, "Are you all right, Jada?"

"Yes, I'm coming." She cleared her throat and turned her attention to rummaging in her closet again, barely tearing herself away from the entrancing sight of her body in the mirror. Her skin was gleaming and perfectly mocha-brown, with no blemishes at all. The mole on her shoulder was gone, as was scar on her knee from the time she had fallen off her bike in third grade.

Even her hair was shiny and flowing, the kinky curls looking as though they'd had a fresh salon treatment. She felt beautiful and amazing, and that brought a load of guilt as she hastily slid on a dress that was now too large before walking—walking, how good that felt—out of the closet and across her bedroom floor on bare feet.

She experienced guilt that her friends were still in various stages of poor health when there was technology to treat them all. She opened the door and took a deep breath before stepping out to join her new alien partner in crime fighting. If that wasn't the strangest turn of events of the day, her physical transformation certainly vied for first.

"This is amazing," she said. "I feel wonderful. I feel better than I ever have in my life, even when I was in my late teens and early twenties and full of energy, before I started getting sick. Thank you for this, Ryland Breese."

"Just Ryland, please." He inclined his head. "I'm happy to see the nanobots were able to communicate with your genetics. It also confirms my theory that women with Kaiser's Syndrome are compatible with Dazon males. Which means..."

"My missing friends and all the other women are probably somewhere at the mercy of your rogue scientist."

He nodded, looking regretful.

"Will he have cured them? If not, can you cure everyone?"

"It's not a cure," he reminded in a gentle tone. Ryland held up a hand, such a human gesture, to indicate he needed her to pause. "I'll assist your friends how I can. I suspect our government will negotiate with your government to trade nanotechnology to keep Kaiser's Syndrome and other illnesses in check in exchange for Earth's government setting up a screening program of women willing to help produce offspring for the Dazon.

"To answer your other question, I have no idea if Dr. Ha would have treated the women, or if he would have left them in a weakened state to make it easier to manipulate them."

Her heart stuttered at the thought, and she took a deep breath in a vain effort to ward off tears that prickled her eyes. "What's he doing to them? Has he been...forcing them and impregnating them?"

Again, Ryland shrugged. "From a logical perspective, the easiest thing to do is accelerate egg production by stimulating the women to produce a larger-than-usual number of eggs. Those would be harvested, fertilized with Dazon sperm, and then grown in an exo-womb. However, I'm uncertain about Dr. Ha, since his ethics are clearly degraded, and he has no respect for the fact that your women are sentient beings with the right to choose for themselves."

His words offered no comfort, but she appreciated the blunt honesty more than she would have a soothing platitude. She stood awkwardly in front of him, finding his height still impressive even now when she was back on her feet and restored to her normal five-seven. Unable to resist the impulse, she reached out and squeezed his hand. "Thank you so much for this, Ryland."

He stiffened lightly at her touch, but he didn't shrug her off. For a moment, she feared she had breached some Dazon etiquette by touching him, and she should regret the impulsive gesture. Instead, her nerve endings sang with sensation. She hadn't experienced such an intense and immediate physical reaction in at least eight years, and probably longer. If ever.

His tawny-gold eyes darkened slightly, and she was certain his breathing pattern changed, but she didn't know what any of that meant. In a human male, they would have been signs of arousal, but she had no way of knowing with an alien.

Regretfully, she forced herself to release him and break the flood of sensation coursing into her. She wondered if it was an actual chemical reaction from touching him, or if it was simply pheromones and attraction. She hugged herself again, tilting her head sideways as she looked up at him. A question suddenly occurred to her. "Why me?"

Ryland frowned. "Why you what, Jada?"

"Why did you pick me to help you? If you needed a human liaison, wouldn't it have been better to pick someone in law enforcement, or even go through proper political channels? I'm no one, so why did you pick me?"

"You had put together enough of the pieces not to freak out—I believe that is the proper phrase—and scream hysterically at the idea of an alien in your house." His answer was perfectly logical, but something about the way he held his shoulders and the rapid movement of his eyes for a moment made her think he hadn't told her the truth, or at least the whole truth.

That raised little alarm bells in the back of her mind, and she cautioned herself to proceed carefully. For the first time since he had offered to heal her, she wondered if he might be affiliated with the people who were taking her friends. Were they sweeping them off their feet with the promise of a cure only to be locked away in some alien harem?

Dread filled her as she realized this could simply be a taste of being healthy. It could be that soon he would present her with the choice of becoming a broodmare in exchange for keeping the technology, or else losing it and reverting back to the wheelchair. Would they consider that honoring the right to choose?

It seemed like wild speculation, but she didn't know the alien in her living room, and she had no way to truly gauge his honesty or intentions. She had to admit it would be a powerful motivator, and if they threatened to take back the gift of health, she would probably be tempted to pump out as many alien babies as they required in order to keep the nanotechnology inside her.

"Now what?" she asked briskly. "How will we find my friends?"

He inclined his head, seeming to be deep in thought for a moment. "There appears to be a geographical pattern to the abductions. They're occurring in a random fashion in each city where they take place, but Dr. Ha and his group are moving steadily around the globe in a semi-predictable manner and have acquired all the women registered with Kaiser's Syndrome, except for those residing in your city. They started in the Far East and have gradually worked their way west since then. Before arriving here, they were in Toronto, where only one woman with Kaiser's Syndrome resides."

"Beautifuleyes_1251."

He arched a brow ridge, looking confused. "Is that an earth idiom?"

She allowed a small smile to blossom despite her distrust. "No, that's one of the members of my board. I bet it's the same person. Beautifuleyes_1251 stopped posting a couple of weeks ago, and she lives in Toronto. All I have for her is an email address, but I traced her through her I.P. number and discovered she's in Toronto. I was able to dig up a phone number for her, but she didn't answer. I hadn't found her cell phone number, and it was on my to-do list of things to accomplish this week."

He looked thoughtful. "There are some things I must check out, and I would suggest you continue your computer probing."

She tried to hide her disappointment, not liking the idea of being banished to the computer once more, though realistically that was her most useful skill, and it made sense to focus on her strengths. It wasn't as though she had any sort of law enforcement or investigative training, unlike the alien inquisitor. She inclined her head to accept his decision before asking, "What are you going to investigate?"

"I'm going to see if there's some kind of holding facility suitable for the doctor's needs. He must be storing the women he's kidnapped, and it seems unlikely he would leave them in a centralized location distant from his current location, especially if he's in the process of egg harvesting or insemination.

"I doubt he's had time to reach the stage of implanting blastocysts into exo-wombs, but if he's farther along than I think, he'll need a place capable of supporting a massive power source, and he'll have arranged some method of travel for the people he's kidnapped."

A pang of worry shot through her, and she couldn't explain it, nor the need to reach out and hold him again, once more grasping his hand with hers. She was startled by her display, but even more startled by the suddenly desperate way he clung to her hand, as though he had been denied physical affection for almost a decade as well.

It was a strange turn of events, but as they held hands and stared into each other's eyes, her heart was pounding in her ears, and a low thrum of desire throbbed through her. For a moment, it threatened to overwhelm her and rob her senses, urging her to leap on the alien and satisfy the surge of lust consuming her.

Remembering her friends, along with all the other women facing an unknown fate, allowed her to regain control and release his hand. "Be careful, Ryland Breese."

He inclined his head in that respectful fashion of his. "And you, Jada Washington. I shall return to you when I have more information."

She nodded and walked him to the door, this time unlocking it the old-fashioned way before locking it behind him. It might not keep out an alien inquisitor, but it would keep out all other manner of criminals and lowlifes plundering the city and perhaps protect her if she became the next target of the alien harvesters.

To her knowledge, there were four cases of Kaiser's Syndrome in the entire state of New York, and three of the women, besides her, lived in the city. The third woman was not a member of the forum, and Jada didn't even know her name. She'd simply seen her at the specialist's office, and they had briefly discussed their diagnoses, but that had been years ago.

The woman had been frail at the time, with dry straw-blonde hair barely touching her neck, and her withered body trapped in a wheelchair. At the time, Jada hadn't even set up her forum yet, and though the conversation they had shared had been informative, part of her had shied away from ever seeing the woman again. At that time, she had been too sharp a predictor of Jada's own future that awaited.

Now, she regretted that she hadn't exchanged some sort of contact information with the woman, and had no idea how to begin tracking her down, unless she went through her doctor's office's electronic records. That felt like a gross invasion of privacy, but it seemed even worse to leave the unidentified woman vulnerable to alien hunters without trying to track her down or warn her. Jada wasn't even sure how she would begin to convince the other woman to take the threat seriously, but she had to at least look for her.

With that thought in mind, she started with the medical records database for her doctor's office. It took a long time to finesse her way through the safeguards, and she was both amused and impressed to find they had better security encryptions than the local police department.

Slowly, she was able to access the system, finally getting full permission to see all the data. She set up a search parameter to look for Kaiser's Syndrome, expecting to get one hit.

The woman she was looking for had been in fairly bad shape eight years ago, so she might have already passed away, but Jada hoped her doctor had converted his old records into electronic records. If so, there should at least be a mention of his former patient, who could still be his current patient.

To her surprise, there were two results for her search for Kaiser's Syndrome. The first file belonged to a Mary Catherine Jones, and she had recently seen Dr. Evans. Jada used her newly restored hands, no longer concerned about pulls and sprains from a simple task like typing or writing, to copy and paste Mary Catherine's contact information onto the computer's notepad. She didn't probe any deeper into the medical records than was necessary to confirm Mary Catherine was probably the person she was looking for.

Curious, she opened the second result, and concern flooded her as she read the case file. It was from a database for AmbaCorp, a medical research group that was connected with the same hospital as her doctor's practice, though located in a different building on the other side of the city. Ostensibly, the study was calling for participants with Kaiser's Syndrome to test an investigational medication meant to reduce excess joint elasticity. Considering Kaiser's Syndrome was barely a blip on the medical radar, it seemed unlikely that a study would be underway to test joint effects, when it was one of the milder side effects of Kaiser's Syndrome.

She dug deeper, looking at the address of the medical research building in question. To her surprise, it wasn't simply an office in the building, but rather took up an entire three-story office building on the outskirts of Brooklyn. Why would a medical research company need such a large facility?

She knew most medical research businesses kept at least a superficial layer between themselves and the manufacturers of the drugs they were testing. They were generally third-party contractors hired to carry out the tests designed by pharmaceutical companies, and she wasn't highly knowledgeable about it, but she'd never heard of people going directly to a lab facility where actual experiments were concurrently conducted in order to participate in a medical study—especially not for a joint medicine.

She made several notes on the notepad document as she waited for Ryland's return, her suspicions growing. Further probing revealed the business was hooked up to public utilities, but had very low power usage compared to most businesses of its size. It took her less than an hour to determine the average usage, and the company was coming nowhere near it.

That was a puzzling contradiction, because Ryland had mentioned specifically that any storage facility would likely require a great deal of electricity. Still, there was enough about the business to be suspicious, and she was impatient for Ryland's return.

As the day dwindled into evening, she looked up when light emanated from her door, and the locks popped open in quick succession. A moment later, the door opened to reveal the alien, and she grinned at him. "You could have rung the bell like normal people, and I would've opened the door for you."

He arched his brow ridge. "I'm not a normal *people*, am I? Besides, I didn't want to alarm you with an unknown presence, so I assumed it would be better to open the door myself."

"I could have been indecent. You might have caught me in a compromising position."

His brow ridge furrowed. "What sort of compromising position?"

She giggled for a moment before the sound choked off. Was she flirting with him? How did one even flirt with an alien who wasn't of one's species? Besides, he probably wouldn't be interested in her.

She waved a hand, hoping to dismiss the whole subject, as something prickled in the back of her mind. She turned to the page she had printed out, about to go over it with him, when the realization flooded her mind.

She might be highly desirable to this alien, because she was a genetic match that could carry his offspring. Even if he wanted nothing more than babies from her, he was likely to be interested and protective. She could use that to her advantage.

She scowled at the thought, shoving it away. She had no intention of using Ryland for anything, whether it be sexual relief or something more mundane. She certainly wasn't going to trick or seduce him into breaking her eight-year dry spell, no matter how much she craved his touch.

It had to be simple proximity. She hadn't been near a man who wasn't a doctor or caregiver in the last seven years, since Barry had bailed. She was in the best health of her life, and it was only normal for her libido to be awake and raring to go after all that time. Any man would have elicited the same response, and he wasn't even a man. He was an alien, for goodness sake. What was she thinking?

"I had some luck, Jada."

Forcing her thoughts to turn from the carnal and back to the business at hand, she grasped the page of notes and turned to face him. "So did I, but tell me what you found first please?"

"New York is full of nooks and crannies, and there are more places to hide a large-scale operation like Dr. Ha might be undertaking than I would have guessed in a city of this geographic size and so filled with a large populace."

She nodded. "New York's a good place to hide secrets, I guess."

"However, I did discover a cargo plane landed at a private airstrip near JFK two weeks ago. Tracing the origins, the same plane has stopped everywhere there have been disappearances, and in the same order as I predict Ha has progressed. Unfortunately, there was no one at the plane or the airfield when I went to investigate, but I have a link, so perhaps I can track down someone in the company and learn more. At least now we know how he's flying them around, so that's progress."

"That's good news. I found something too." She handed him the page. "You can read English, right?"

"My translator can rapidly translate it for me. I don't actually speak, read, or write English, but I doubt you can tell the difference or detect the slight delay from the translator changing my words to the right form for you."

"Oh, okay. Anyway, I knew there was at least one other woman with Kaiser's Syndrome in the city. I set out to track her down, since we share a doctor. In the process, I discovered she's still alive, and our doctor recommended her for a study for a medication that will reduce overextension of the joints in Kaiser's patients. She's been enrolled, and when she went to the program four days ago, she hasn't been seen since.

"There have been no hits on her credit card or debit card, and from what I could tell from her landline, she's had a few incoming phone calls, but has placed no outgoing calls. Most of the calls last less than a minute, suggesting the caller is leaving a message.

"I also checked delivery records for restaurants nearby, assuming she has the same culinary weaknesses of the rest of us, and discovered she's a fan of Thai food, ordering it at least twice a week, but nothing at all in the last four days."

"This is Mary Catherine Jones of whom you speak?" At her nod, his gaze moved lower down the page. "And you suspect the study is a front for Dr. Ha to acquire Kaiser's patients?"

She lifted a shoulder. "It makes sense, except for electricity usage. It's too low for a business that size, even if they're doing nothing more than running conference rooms and doing basic labs studies—which if that's all they're doing, why do they need a fifteen thousand square-feet facility with three floors?"

Ryland inclined his head. "It's a very large space for one business of that type, but would provide ideal quarters if you're trying to hold four hundred women, and you needed a floor for medical research, another for housing prisoners, and a third to act as the front to lure in more patients. It's also unlikely he would rely on a human power source to keep the facility running. Dazon technology is more efficient and highly portable."

"I was thinking tomorrow I should go check it out."

Ryland stiffened. "What?"

She tilted her head. "It makes perfect sense. I have Kaiser's Syndrome, so it gives me a good reason to snoop around a bit. I don't have to commit to joining their study, but I can see the layout and try to determine if it's just a medical research facility, or if there's something more going on."

Ryland crossed his arms over his chest, and his fierce scowl was hot enough to melt off the top layer of her skin. "Absolutely not. Do you know how dangerous that will be?"

She nodded. "I'm aware, but it'll be much easier for me to get in than it would be for you. I actually have the disease."

He shook his head again. "I won't risk losing you. I've looked too long—" He broke off, his eyes stormy, and his expression revealing nothing but stubborn resistance. "It's out of the question."

She shook her head at him. "You came to me for help. This is how I can do that."

"Absolutely not," he roared again. "I won't lose my mate after searching so long for you, certain I would never find you."

"You're being unreasonable. I'm perfectly capable of..." She trailed off as his words penetrated the haze in her brain. "What are you talking about? I'm not your mate." She shook her head. "I barely know you."

Ryland sighed, rubbing a hand down his perfectly sculpted face in a weary gesture that was surprisingly human. "Our people have a finely developed mating instinct."

"You mean a healthy sex drive?"

He made a sound that could have been a snort or a laugh. "Yes, I suppose we have that as well, but I mean we have an instinct inside us, one science has never fully explained, that guides us to our intended mate. In many of the men born today, the instinct is dormant, and our scientists have begun to believe we've evolved past it due to a lack of females to keep it active.

"Perhaps it could be due to the genetic tampering of our scientists that allow any reproduction at all as well. Whatever the cause, it's mostly regarded as an old-fashioned or out-of-place ability. I considered it the same, until I saw your picture. I didn't have the mating flare, but I felt something that instinctively told me I would when I saw you in person and not just from a picture."

She frowned. "When you saw my blog, you mean?"

He hesitated before shaking his head. "No, I saw you before then. When I first suspected Dr. Ha had gone rogue to undertake his operation, I tracked down all the known Earth women with Kaiser's Syndrome."

He shook his head. "No, that's not quite right. More than a dozen women had already disappeared, coinciding with his known whereabouts on his supposed hiatus, and when I realized they all had a genetic mutation that he had described as ideal for our genetics in his last reports before taking time off 'to rest,' I determined the location of the others."

Confusion filled her. "Wait? Were you watching Dr. Ha before he started kidnapping women?"

Ryland nodded once. "I was assigned the duty. My superior felt it prudent, considering Dr. Ha's publicly stated leanings toward coercion and kidnapping of compatible species—especially if they were technologically inferior to us and couldn't offer a meaningful resistance."

She frowned at him. "So you knew all the women at risk, and you didn't warn them?"

He hesitated again before sighing. "I wanted to, but the decision was made by the High Council that we would simply observe and intercede when the timing was right." He scowled, and a look of disgust crept over his face. "It's my belief there are enough people on the High Council who wanted to see Dr. Ha's results that they deliberately dragged their feet, though that action is contrary to the decision reached by the General Council, with input offered by every Dazon."

She softened slightly toward him. "Are you the only one assigned to this case?"

Ryland paused, nodded, and then paused again before shaking his head. "I am assigned, but I'm not authorized to act directly. I'm supposed to be observing, but when I realized they were moving into New York, I knew I had to protect you. When you posted your blog article, it gave me the perfect opening to approach you without arousing suspicion or drawing Ha's attention if he has someone on the Council supporting his research. If Jorvak knows you're my mate, it might make him more determined than ever to take you."

She ignored the bit about being his mate for a moment to focus on the question burning on the tip of her tongue. "Why would that be? Does he know you personally?"

Ryland nodded. "Quite personally. We have the same genetic father, though we were grown in exo-wombs several cycles apart."

Her mouth dropped open. "He's your brother?"

Ryland paused, as though processing an answer. "I suppose from a human definition, he would be my half-brother, but due to our scientists' manipulation, we're actually more like eighty percent of our father, and only about twenty percent of the genetic material contributed by the Dazon female who mothered us. We had separate donor mothers, in an attempt to maintain genetic diversity as much as possible."

She rubbed her brow as she tried to absorb his words, her kinky curls clinging to her hand in the process. She shoved them away with an impatient flick of her hand. "So why would he be interested because you're involved?" She absolutely wasn't going to utter anything about being his mate. Jada wasn't going to indulge the delusion—or admit to herself how much she liked the idea, though it was completely implausible and ridiculous.

"Jorvak will dismiss most unscientific things, but if he knows I've experienced the mating flare when I first saw you, he'll know you're a close genetic match for me, so you're likely to be for him as well. It will make the creation of offspring that much easier, and he's likely to want to claim you for his mate, not just as another source of eggs for harvesting."

"Oh, goodie." She gave a sharp little laugh. "It's strictly a genetic thing, not because you guys are blood enemies or something then?"

He shook his head. "Jorvak and I have very little communication or interface, Jada. Familial bonds are not the same in recent generations. They can't be due to the changes in our world and the loss of females."

She let out a heavy sigh. "I hope you aren't planning to persuade all the Earth women to donate genetic material to raise children with that information. It all sounds so sterile, and you aren't even really family anymore. Most women aren't going to go for that."

He took a step toward her, and his legs were so long that the single step swallowed most of the space remaining between them. "Then perhaps you will tell me what most Earth women would *go for*, Jada?"

It was an innocuous question, but the smoky tint to his voice rendered it something altogether different. Her nipples hardened against the fabric of her oversized dress, and she struggled for a moment to draw in a deep breath as his physical proximity struck her.

"Earth women want love. They'll want to be cherished and have an equal partnership, to know the union is more than just some sort of reproductive act. They're also going to want to be involved with raising their offspring. Most women, and men for that matter, are hardwired to care for our young. You aren't going to find many women who will voluntarily hand over their eggs and not care about the outcome, or the child that could result.

"I don't know what your people have planned, but if you really want this to be a consensual arrangement, you're going to have to change your presentation and offer the women of Earth something more than a cold, scientific contract."

He lifted a hand and hovered near her cheek without quite touching. "What should we offer them, Jada?"

"You should offer to get to know her, and to take her out and become well acquainted with the woman you plan to mate."

"And if the mating instinct burns brighter when you touch her?" He cupped her cheek as he asked the question, his fingers lightly grazing her skin. "If it feels like your hearts will pound out of your chest, and you will die if you don't have her right that minute, will an Earth woman understand the frantic need and allow a Dazon male to bypass some of the courtship rites?"

She licked her lips as her heart raced even faster in her ears. "It depends on the woman, I guess. Some women are going to want a traditional approach, while other women are more likely to be influenced by a physical response." As she uttered the last words, she swayed closer to him, until her beaded nipples pressed against the slippery cloth of his black bodysuit.

His entire body seem to hum with warmth, and it was making her body temperature rise as well. It also brought a slick wave of molten heat between her legs, and she whimpered as she lifted her hands to grasp his shoulders. "Sometimes, you'll find a woman who's surprisingly okay with a one-night stand, even if she's not agreeing to be a mate for life."

He frowned. "Under the influence of the mating instinct, I can't imagine anything but mating for life." As he spoke the last words, his head dipped, and his lips approached hers.

It was all her, and all her choice, when she stretched to close the distance between them and pressed her lips to his. The kiss was intense and explosive, hotter than anything she'd ever known, and her already-racing heart galloped into full speed as she wrapped her arms tightly around him, and he embraced her tightly.

His mouth devoured hers, first with extreme precision before becoming less coordinated and more frantic rather than thoughtful. She was aware of doing the same, of frenzied need beating through her, and the heat of desire pulsing between her legs that urged her to seek relief with the man in her arms.

Alien, whispered a dim voice of the back of her mind, but it barely registered and didn't matter. She couldn't imagine any circumstances under which she would lose all desire for him. Perhaps if his golden form melted away to reveal a gelatinous blob with multiple tentacles, she might tear herself away and ran out screaming, but that seemed unlikely.

Partially to reassure herself, and also because she suddenly needed to breathe, she pulled her mouth away from his. "Is this your real form?"

Ryland nodded. "This is my species' natural appearance, though there are variations in skin tone, eye color, and shade of hair."

"So there're no surprises, like tentacles underneath, or anything else weird?"

He pressed his forehead to hers as he laughed. "No unpleasant surprises, though I am anatomically different from human males."

Her stomach rippled with dread. "How? How different?"

He hesitated for a moment before stepping back from her. She felt bereft without his arms around her, but was curious enough to fight back the compulsion to follow and wrap her arms around him again.

He pressed something on the neck of his garment, and it flickered like the Mr. Bland illusion earlier, before disappearing. Once the black garment was gone, or rendered invisible, or teleported to the ninth quadrant of the Gamma galaxy for all she knew, he was completely naked and bare to her visual inspection.

His body was as toned and perfect as the tight-fitting suit had suggested, but it hadn't revealed his genitalia before. She watched with surprise and awe as his shaft, which had lain dormant against his leg, thickened and sprouted upward.

He was larger than the average Earth man, but not so large as to be frightening or make her think there was no way she could physically accept him. Moved by her curiosity, she dropped to her knees to inspect him more closely. She peered up at him through the veil of her curls before blowing them out of the way with an upward gust of air through her lips. "Is it all right if I touch you?"

His face spasmed in what seemed like agony, but he nodded in an eager fashion. "Please."

She brought a hand to his shaft, drawing her fingers lightly over the silken skin. He hissed at the first touch of her fingers against him, and she looked up, seeing more of that pleasure/pain expression on his face. She hesitated. "Am I hurting you?"

He shook his head. "No, it just feels amazing. Better than I ever dreamed it would."

Tentatively, she wrapped her hand around him and stroked up and down, trying to find his most sensitive spots. On a human male, it would be on the underside of the head, but he didn't have that kind of anatomy.

The shaft was smooth and long, perfectly cylindrical with a rounded tip, and there was a small slit at the end. He produced a clear fluid, though it had a hint of golden bioluminescence to it, and she couldn't resist the urge to bend forward and extend her tongue, running it lightly over the tip of him to taste his arousal.

Ryland's pre-cum was thinner than she remembered a human male's being, but much sweeter. It wasn't a fruity or a candy type of sweetness. It was simply indescribable, but syrupy and delicious. Drawing back, she looked up at him to tease gently, "Perhaps you won't have to woo the Earth women after all. If they know how good you taste, they might come supplicating to you on their knees just to drain you dry."

His skin seemed to flicker, going from light golden-brown to deep bronze for a moment. It was a whole-body effect, but it reminded her of a flush. Was he a little shy about such things? Remembering his comment about it being better than he'd expected, something clicked. "Um, Ryland?"

"Yes, Jada?" His expression was contorted, and his fists clenched tightly at his sides, as though he was barely hanging on to his last shred of control.

"Have you ever done this before?"

He shook his head, gnashing his teeth together for a moment as the chords in his neck tightened. "Females spend their fertile years procreating in breeding facilities, and none of them mate until their fertility has dwindled. At that point, the highest ranking officials are entitled to offer for them, to care for the females through retirement until death, but the average male doesn't have a female partner."

She paused to swirl her tongue around the tip of his penis again, unable to resist sucking for a moment to draw out his sweet fluid. His harsh groan of pleasure also increased her own, and it was difficult to tear herself away to continue the conversation. "What about with each other? Do Dazon men mate with each other?"

"It's become more common from necessity, but many would still prefer a female mate."

She hesitated. "Do you have a boyfriend or something?" She wasn't going to be a cheater, even if it wasn't considered cheating in his society.

He shook his head. "I experimented a bit as a youngling, but it always felt hollow. It wasn't what I wanted, or what I craved. There was little difference between pleasuring myself or being pleasured by a partner. Without the mating flare and that intense emotional experience, it's simply a different form of physical release, and it wasn't enough for me, so I chose celibacy and self-pleasure."

She nodded, understanding that. While she had never experimented with anyone from the same gender, she had certainly had her share of disappointing lovers, often reaching the conclusion it was simpler just to stay home with her vibrator than try to go out and meet another disappointment. Even Barry, whom she had planned to marry, had been only all right in bed, but nothing spectacular. He'd seemingly had so many other things going for him—stability, a grounded outlook, and readiness for a family—that she had considered the sex part unimportant.

Now she considered herself an idiot for ever thinking that way, and it wasn't just because she'd discovered the truth about Barry. After going eight years without sex, she'd come to realize how much she'd missed it and how much she deserved really good sex.

She had a strong feeling Ryland could certainly provide that. He just might need a little coaxing or coaching. She licked his smooth shaft again before asking, "How far did your experimentation go? Has anyone done this before?" Jada rolled her tongue around the tip of his shaft to punctuate the question.

He groaned and arched his hips forward before saying, "No," in a choked voice.

It was a little intimidating to be his first, but also endearing and sweetly sexy. Determined to give him pleasure, she opened her mouth as wide as she could and slowly sucked his cock inside. He moaned, and his entire body spasmed as his hands gripped her hair tightly in what seemed to be an instinctive reaction.

She withdrew before sliding her mouth down again, taking as much of him as she could until he breached the back of her throat and reached her limits. She ran her hand up and down the exposed root of his erection, the part where her mouth wouldn't reach, as she enthusiastically sucked and bobbed her head. His taste was addictive, but his responses were even more so. He looked like he was almost in pain from the amount of pleasure he was feeling.

With a guttural ground, his hand tightened in her hair, and he pushed her closer to him seconds before his shaft spasmed between her lips, and more of his sweet nectar flowed into her mouth and down her throat. She drank all of it down, sucking lightly to coax more from him until he sagged forward, clearly spent for the moment.

Carefully, she disengaged, making certain she didn't scrape him with her teeth as she pulled back and sat on her calves, looking up at him. "Did you enjoy that?"

The hand holding her hair loosened, and now he started stroking her thick ringlets instead of holding them. "It was amazing. Thank you, Jada."

She smiled him at him and took the hand he extended to help her to her feet. He was completely naked, and she was still fully dressed. It was a little unnerving, and she felt oddly vulnerable even though she was the one wearing her clothes. "How do your people mate?"

"Like yours." His eyes had darkened to the shade of burnt honey, and his skin was definitely a darker golden than it had been before the blowjob.

He bent his head to kiss her again, and she offered up her mouth willingly, their tongues stroking each other. His hands roamed over her body, and she pressed closer to him in her eagerness to feel her skin against his. It might have been his first time with a woman, but he seemed to know what he was doing by the way he stripped her clothes with no fumbling, even mastering the hook on her bra his first try.

"I want to take you to your bedroom now. May I, Jada?"

With a nod, she took his hand to lead him there. She managed to take two steps before he picked her up and whisked her the rest of the way down the hallway and through her bedroom door, closing it behind him with his foot. He laid her on the bed, draping her so that her legs were splayed, and her arms were widely spaced and elbows tucked behind her.

He joined her on the bed a moment later, his fingers playing with the elastic band of her underwear, which was the only garment she still wore. She regretted they were plain white cotton, but he didn't seem to care.

His head dipped lower, and his golden tongue slipped from his mouth to trace around her nut-brown nipple, savoring the succulent bud and tightening it almost to the point of pain. He flicked his tongue across the tip before taking it into his mouth and sucking firmly.

A new surge of moisture filled her folds, and she arched her hips restlessly in search of relief. His fingers dipped into the waistband of her panties, gliding over her soft skin and rounded tummy to find her mound. He stroked the thatch of curls before parting them to seek out her slit.

"Yes, just like that. Touch me please, Ryland." She bit back a whimper as his fingers slipped inside her folds, tracing her interior anatomy with an air of experimentation, as though he was both aroused and curious. She had experienced something similar at the first sight of his cock, so she imagined it was the same for him.

She arched her hips and circled slightly, deliberately bringing his fingers against her clitoris. "Stroke me there please."

He circled his fingers around the spasming bud, making her draw in a deep breath each time he made a rotation. His mouth moved to her other breast, worshiping it with equal attention, and she shut off her brain, surrendering to the sensations sweeping through her.

Her core contracted as she came, drenching his fingers with her slick release, and she moaned at the sight of Ryland dipping his head, his tongue flicking out before she lost sight of the appendage as it moved lower. All she could see then was his hair between her legs while he stripped off her panties, before his tongue slipped inside her, probing her depths and homing in on her clit.

She was still sensitive from the first orgasm, and his experimental suck of the taut bud caused another to overtake her, one so intense that she screamed out her release and wriggled backward from his questing mouth in an attempt to escape the almost-pain of his intimate kiss.

Ryland looked up at her uncertainly as she moved back from him a bit, his brow ridge furrowed. "Are you all right, Jada? Have I done something wrong?"

She shook her head, not able to answer for a moment while she gathered her composure with several deep breaths. "No, you did everything right. It was really good actually. I just got so sensitive, and it was starting to hurt a little bit."

He nodded. "It's the same for me. As I'm straining to climax, there's some…pain almost, and then it's completely obliterated when I release."

She scooted down the bed again, bringing herself close to him as she grasped his erection in her palm, guiding him toward her aching slit. "It sounds like we have a lot in common then."

He nodded, his expression a blend of interest, arousal, and perhaps a hint of uncertainty as she directed him to lie on his back and straddled him. "It makes sense, since we're a close genetic match."

She nodded, but didn't pursue the line of conversation. The last thing she wanted to do was think about genetics and scientific probabilities at the moment, when she was far more interested in more visceral experiences.

Grasping his smooth shaft, she guided it toward her sheath, bracing herself for pain as he slowly breached her tightly closed channel. After seven years without so much as an orgasm, because she'd had no sex drive, and certainly no penetration, she anticipated his possession would be uncomfortable.

She let out a sharp exhalation when his cock stretched her, slowly pushing its way in as she sank down the length of him. Her body was resistant for a moment, but adjusted to the intrusion with surprising rapidity. Soon, she was able to withdraw and sink down on him again.

His fingers dug into her hips, and he was helping to lift her up and practically slamming her down on him as they fucked with enthusiasm. It was the enthusiasm of virgins, because he had never been with a woman before, and she was practically a virgin after her eight years of celibacy.

As her sheath contracted around him, and he twitched inside her, she vaguely realized they probably should have used some type of protection, since they were a close genetic match. Surely, it would require some sort of laboratory assistance for them to create a child, since they weren't an exact genetic match?

If not, she was beyond caring. The idea of having his child didn't scare her. It actually sent a surge of warmth through her, and as she attained physical release, emotional satisfaction filled her at the idea of being a mother, especially the mother of his children. It was a dream she had tried to let go of years ago, knowing it was impossible. Now, thanks to him, it was no longer an impossibility, and after their intense lovemaking, it might be far closer to a certainty.

Afterward, they laid together on her bed, her head on his chest, with her cheek pressed against his rib cage, and her ear nestled to his thumping heartbeat, which seemed twice as fast as hers. She had never felt so content, and she wanted to tell him that, but she was too lethargic from extreme pleasure to speak at the moment. Instead, sleep crept over her stealthily, and she reminded herself to tell him what this had meant to her in the morning when they woke.

Chapter Four

SHE WOKE ALONE. AFTER eight years of sleeping with no one else, perhaps it should have felt completely natural to her, but it didn't. She was bereft even before she opened her eyes, and as she stretched out her hand to feel the cold bed beside her, she knew he was gone and had been for hours.

Reluctantly, she forced her eyes open and frowned at the ceiling as she wondered why he had left. She didn't think he was gone for good, but she wished he had taken a moment to wake her and explain why he was leaving.

Her lips tightened, and she cursed aloud as she realized he had probably slipped away with the intention of investigating AmbaCorp alone, not wanting to endanger her.

Anger swept through her, and her first impulse was to jump from the bed and make her way to the medical research facility to investigate, as she had planned. However, a deep breath brought a return of logic, and she acknowledged that perhaps he had a point about her investigating. She wasn't trained to do so, and she couldn't really defend herself if it became physical.

Abruptly, she remembered Mary Catherine Jones had entered the facility five days ago, and no one had heard from her since. Her ambitious, but naïve, plan to have a look around and poke through things seemed shortsighted now, and she reluctantly admitted to herself Ryland had been right to reject the idea—though not right to arbitrarily make the decision for her and creep out early in the morning before she awoke.

When he returned, she intended to tell him strongly that she didn't like him slipping away and completely taking the decision from her. Now that she was fully functioning once more, she wanted to be useful and actually live again.

That didn't mean she wanted to throw herself back into an intense social life, or make small talk with a bunch of strangers. She simply wanted to find a balance between being stuck in the apartment and being forced to go out for every little thing. Now that she could choose again, she demanded she retain that ability. Most of all, she wanted to find a place for Ryland in her new life as she figured out the direction she was going to take.

She wasn't completely sold on the mating flare thing he talked about, and she didn't believe in soulmates, but she was willing to keep an open mind and see how the relationship progressed. What kind of future was there with a seven-foot alien who couldn't go out in public without wearing his Mr. Bland disguise? She didn't know, and it was something they would have to address after they tracked down the missing women and stopped the rogue scientist.

After a quick shower, she made her way to the kitchen to have a bite to eat. Following her vigorous night in his arms, her body was screaming for sustenance.

She was finally mollified when she found a note pinned to her refrigerator, written in very precise handwriting. The message was succinct:

I've gone to investigate AmbaCorp. I'm not going inside at the moment, but will later this evening. In the meantime, could you find schematics for the business? That will be helpful for me tonight.

R

He hadn't even taken time to sign his full name, but she took that as a good sign. She would obviously know who he was, and the simple initial seemed more intimate somehow than his full name would have been, especially if he had added his surname.

Was that what aliens called their last name? He'd introduced himself as Ryland Breese, and she couldn't help testing it out in her mind. Jada Breese. It sounded nice, but she shook her head at her own silliness and forced her attention to finishing the toast and cereal before moving to the computer to accomplish the task he'd requested.

She suspected this was along the lines of busywork, because he considered it safe for her to stay at her computer and find information for him. Surely, he must have some sort of scanning device or advanced binoculars that would have allowed him to see the layout of the building from the exterior, but just in case it wasn't simply a task he'd assigned so she would feel like she was contributing, she needed to get to work.

She grimaced as she sank into the wheelchair again, hating it with every fiber of her being now that she was freed from the contraption. She never would have sat in it again, but her house was woefully under-furnished, and it was the only seat available at the computer table. She didn't have a laptop, because she hadn't been mobile enough to move it around her house before the nanobots, so she would just have to sit in the chair, but she vowed it would be the last time. Sometime today, she would find a way to get a new chair, and perhaps some other new furniture.

She was deep in the files of the City Planning database when the door hummed, and light emanated from it. She didn't bother to look up, not wanting to lose the data packet she was following, as she waited for Ryland to enter.

The locks popped, and the door swung open. Almost immediately, she knew it wasn't Ryland stepping into her space. She wasn't certain how she knew that, but the person felt wrong to her.

She looked up from her computer with dread and fear as she saw two people step into her apartment, both wearing black suits and looking very nondescript. She immediately recognized them as Mr. Bland disguises, and her first impulse was to push up from the chair and run for it.

As they approached, she froze. She appeared to be paralyzed with fright, and though she wasn't that good of an actress—she was certainly terrified—she wasn't completely incapacitated by terror either. It occurred to her as the two aliens approached, their expressions revealing nothing, that it was to her benefit to appear to still be confined to the chair.

If they realized she had been healed, they would know someone was on to them, though they might not know it was Ryland directly. She would be putting her lover at risk, along with herself. Either way, she didn't think she could fight them off, so they were going to take her. This way, they would be lax about security if they thought she was immobilized.

As they approached, she pressed her back into the chair and lifted her hands. "Who are you? What do you want?"

"Remain calm, Jada Washington," said Left Mr. Bland.

"You've been recruited for a medical study," said Right Mr. Bland as they boxed her in.

Her heart was racing in her ears, and she didn't have to fake the note of fear that made her voice shake. "What are you doing with me?"

Neither bothered to answer her as they stood on either side of her chair, both men taking an arm of the wheelchair in one hand and hefting it, and her, seemingly with no difficulty at all. The show of strength was frightening and demoralizing, and she didn't know if it was a deliberate display, or if they were simply no-nonsense in their collection practices. After four hundred women, they probably had their routine down pretty well, after all.

As they walked past it, she managed to hit the button to turn off her computer, just in case they decided to look at her screen. Neither man seemed at all interested in it, and she was relieved. Otherwise, they would have seen just exactly what she was digging for in the City

Planning Department's database. That would have led to questions about why she wanted schematics for the building housing AmbaCorp, which was likely just a front for the alien kidnapping and breeding ring led by the mysterious Dr. Ha.

Unfortunately for her, he was about to become far more known and less mysterious, since the doctor had clearly decided to enroll her in his so-called study. Jada was sure Dr. Ha was studying the women he'd stolen, but not in a benign fashion, and certainly not in a way that would benefit anyone with Kaiser's Syndrome. She wasn't entirely faking it when she whimpered and allowed some of her fear to show, which made her shake in the chair.

She hoped Ryland would return soon. When he saw the wheelchair gone, would he realize what had happened? Surely he would know she wouldn't have voluntarily taken it anywhere, and with the locks off the door, though there was no damage to them, he would surely comprehend someone had let themselves into her apartment and taken her. Once he came to that conclusion, he would immediately understand it was his half-brother and come for her.

"Where are you taking me?" she asked as they loaded her wheelchair into the van, securing her chair with straps. It was akin to the bus for the disabled that she often took to doctor's appointments or scheduled to go shopping, but when they closed the door without answering, she saw there were no handles on the inside. Only they could let her out.

She hoped when Ryland came for her that he was able to do so safely, and he wouldn't be alone. She didn't like the idea of him facing who knew how many, all of them aliens like him, which diminished the physical advantage he would have had over human assailants.

"Hurry up, Ryland," she whispered softly, allowing herself the comfort of speaking his name just once before she subsided into silence. Once she was at the facility, she would have to pretend like she had never heard of Ryland, and she would have to slip back into the invalid role, though it didn't sit well with her.

It was ironic that the device which had been her virtual prison for the last seven years was now one of the things that might end up saving her. The wheelchair was oddly comforting, or at least what it represented, as the van drove farther from her home and contact with Ryland.

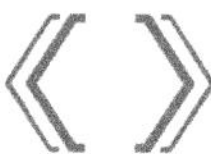

WHEN THE VAN STOPPED, Jada clung to the arms of the wheelchair and debated her chances of making a run for it despite her earlier plan. As the doors opened, the same two Mr. Blands stood there, but there were two more behind them, and she hesitated, perhaps too long to act, because the first two who had kidnapped her stepped into the van and unfastened the strap around her chair to wheel her down the ramp that folded from the van.

She looked at them closely, searching for any sign of their true alien form, but their disguises were perfect, other than the fact that they looked almost identical. So did the other two as she got nearer, and she stiffened when one of them put a hand on her shoulder and gave her what was supposed to be a reassuring smile, though it simply sent chills racing up her spine.

"Welcome to the program, Jada Washington." The fourth alien held the door open, and they slipped inside the back entrance of a large building, which she presumed was AmbaCorp, moving in procession, with one of the aliens pushing her chair, another one walking farther ahead, the fourth bringing up the rear, and the one who still had his creepy hand on her shoulder walking alongside as he looked down at her.

She shuddered when his Mr. Bland disguised melted to become his true form. Almost immediately, she knew this had to be Ryland's half-brother, Jorvak Ha. They shared some resemblance, though Ha's features were rougher and more irregular. She grimaced in disgust.

He must have mistaken her reaction for fear of his alien visage, which was a relief since she wasn't supposed to know about his existence.

He patted her shoulder in a reassuring fashion. "I know this seems frightening, Jada, but you have no reason to fear us. We need something from you, and in the end, we'll ensure you're healthy again."

She stiffened, glaring up at him. "What do you want from me?"

"There's something very unique about you, and the other women like you, and our species requires your assistance."

She knew exactly what he was talking about, but she couldn't betray that knowledge. Instead, she forced a deadpan expression. "I've been told I'm a heckuva blogger, and I'm pretty gifted with hacking, though I'd appreciate you not telling anyone about that, so if you need either one of those skills, I'm the person for you. You could have just called me like normal...er, aliens?"

His expression remained unchanged, so either he had no sense of humor, or she just wasn't funny. "I'm afraid we need something more...fundamental from you and your compatriots."

She crossed her arms over her chest. "Like what? I'd like some answers before I go any farther."

The doctor patted her arm in a condescending fashion before finally removing his hand from her. "I'm afraid it doesn't really matter what you want at this point, Jada. You've been recruited for a great honor, and a great duty. Our people will revere your contribution."

"That's terrific," she said darkly. "Am I going to be alive to see this great reverence, Doctor?" She cursed herself for uttering the slip even as he stiffened. "Or am I wrong in guessing you're a mad scientist-type?" She held her breath as she waited to see if he would accept her attempts to cover her slipup without suspicion.

After a moment, he simply gave her a brief nod. "I am a doctor, though hardly a mad scientist. I'm a revolutionary genius on my planet, though many do not yet recognize that. They will when we prove our success though. Oh yes, they will."

Great. He wasn't a dedicated scientist. Instead, he was after the glory too. At least if he had been doing this horrible experiment strictly to save his people, it would have been slightly preferable. Not that there was any justification for kidnapping and forcibly harvesting genetic material from four hundred people, but it was even more reprehensible to know he was doing it for some sort of accolade by the Dazon. "And if I'd prefer to decline this honor?"

He shook his head, his expression completely cold, though his tone was warmly sympathetic. "I'm afraid that isn't an option, Jada. I must leave you now, but my assistants will see that you're settled in after intake testing."

She stiffened again, her breath catching in her throat as she realized they planned to start right away. Fear nearly blinded her, because she was terrified of what they might do to her. As the doctor left them, and they detoured to the left down the hallway, she clenched her hands around the wheelchair as an even graver possibility occurred to her.

What if they detected the nanobots in her bloodstream and realized she had a connection to one of their own? Or at least one of their own species, but not their group. How would they react? She wasn't certain, but at the very least, it would remove Ryland's ability to stage a surprise attack.

She was close to hyperventilating by the time they stopped before a hydraulic door, and one of the aliens pressed a button on a metal pad by the wall to allow their entry. It was a cold and sterile room, filled with medical instruments and a large table in the middle that sent a shudder of dread down her spine when she saw the straps attached to it.

She had known intellectually that they didn't care about the women they were compulsorily recruiting, but seeing the reality up close and personally of just how ruthless and uncaring they were brought it home sharply. She and the other women like her were little more than lab rats to these people, to be confined and used as needed.

She didn't believe Dr. Ha's promise about healing them when it was over. It was far more likely he would harvest everything useful from the lot of them and dispose of all the women, or simply leave them here in this warehouse facility to rot when he returned to Dazonia Major.

She almost resisted on pure instinct when the two aliens still acting as her escorts came to her chair and took her arm, one on each side. At the last second, she realized if she was strapped into that bed, she would be completely at their mercy. If she remained passive and docile, and they believed she was too feeble to attempt an escape, perhaps she could persuade them not to fasten the straps.

It was a risky proposition, but perhaps it would buy her some time. At the moment, the aliens probably weren't looking for her to fight them off and run away, so she had the element of surprise on her side if she acted. The major flaw in that plan was the fact that she had no idea how to fight them off. They would have to be incapacitated, or they would alert the facility to her attempted escape. More likely, they would both, in conjunction, easily subdue her, and that would be the end of any possibility of escape.

By the time she had settled on the least terrible of her two options, they had carried her and lifted her to the table/bed/chair, because it appeared to be able to form multiple positions as she saw from the joints and odd angles when they got her closer to it.

They were gentle with her when they put her on the bed, but it wasn't in a thoughtful way. It was more like the way one would handle an expensive object they didn't want to break, and not because they had any concern for actually hurting her personally.

One of the former Mr. Blands lifted the set of straps on his side, bringing them to her wrist. She pulled her arm away, shaking her head. "That's hardly necessary. I assume you've seen my medical file? I can't walk anywhere by myself for more than two or three steps. Where am I going to go, E.T.?"

The alien grunted and looked at his companion, who shrugged. After a moment, they dropped the straps, allowing Jada to breathe just a bit easier as a surge of relief swept through her. It was a minor victory, absolutely minuscule in comparison to what she still had to accomplish if she wanted to survive this, but she was thankful for at least one thing going the way she had hoped.

"I can handle this, Tredor." The alien on her left nodded to the other alien before stepping back from her. He didn't speak as he let himself out of the room, and she dared cling to that as another bit of good luck. Assuming he didn't come back, it would be just her against one alien for now. Those were still intimidating odds, but she was more likely to succeed in a one-on-one situation.

She tried to remain passive, waiting for the right moment, as the alien assistant bustled around her, hooking her up to machines and getting readings from things she had no idea how to interpret. She was successful in remaining quiet until the alien brought out a deceptively simple-looking device, similar to a screwdriver, though without the metal tip. It was more like the handle of the screwdriver, though not as ergonomically shaped for a human hand. She tensed as he got closer, holding another shiny metal object in his other hand. "What are you going to do to me?"

"I need a tissue sample, Ms. Washington."

Her eyes widened as he lifted the cylindrical object and brought it closer to the outside of her bicep. "And just how do you plan to obtain it?"

"This will numb the area." He held up the can before spraying it on her arm. And then he held up the other device that was so ominously nondescript. "And this will allow me to take a sample." He pressed a button, and a short laser beam shot out of it. She stiffened and tried to scoot farther away from him, pressing her back against the table. "Not with that pygmy light saber, you aren't."

The alien arched a brow ridge, looking completely befuddled. "This device is a laser scalpel, Ms. Washington, and you'll feel nothing, I assure you."

Since she still didn't have a weapon or a plan, she closed her eyes and barely bit back a whimper as the alien brought his laser scalpel against her skin. A second later, the unpleasant scent of burning flesh filled the immediate area, but there was no pain.

She dared to look down in time to see a big chunk of her flesh and muscle disappearing into a metal basin. Her stomach clenched with nausea when she saw the gaping wound, and she didn't have to fake the impulse to vomit. She simply bent over to the left side and hurled.

The alien made a sound that could have been exasperation or concern, and he quickly set down his implements on a stand near him. It looked like the same kind of metal tray that her doctor's office used, and she wondered if they had outfitted AmbaCorp with human technology that was readily available, or if there were just some commonalities across their species. The first idea seemed more likely.

As the alien walked around the table to deal with her mess, she was pleased to see he hadn't taken time to put away the numbing spray or the laser scalpel. Cautiously, she reached for them one at a time with her right arm, pressing them close to her thigh in an attempt to shield her possession of them from his gaze. She didn't dare risk using her left arm since he was so close to that side of her.

He was too far away for her to practically stab him with the laser scalpel before he would realize what was occurring. Instead, she reclined with rigid posture, her hand curled around the laser scalpel as she waited for an opportunity.

When it came, it was unexpectedly the numbing agent she used first. The alien had crouched down on his hands and knees to clean up the vomit, and as he started to rise after finishing the unpleasant task, his eyes were level with the bed. Acting more on instinct than cool intellect or logic, she released her hold on the laser scalpel and brought up the numbing agent, spraying it all in his eyes. She doubted it would hurt, but hoped it would blind him.

He reeled back and said a word she didn't recognize, so she assumed his translation system must not have anything even close to the word in English. It was probably an alien curse word.

Before he could get too far away, she dropped the numbing agent and lifted the laser scalpel instead, bringing it up and clicking the button as he had done. For a moment, the laser beam flickered before fading away. Her heart was racing in her ears, and the alien seemed to be less jerky in his motions, which meant he was probably rapidly recovering from any effects of the numbing agent. She pressed the button again, harder this time, and the short laser beam shot out.

As he reached for her, she slid off the table and ducked under his arm, moving around behind him to stab the scalpel through his back with a sweeping slice. The laser burned through his flesh easily, and that same unpleasant odor of charred flesh filled the air, once again making her want to vomit. Instead, she pulled out the scalpel and shoved it back in, this time a direct puncture wound into the back of his neck, where the brain stem would be on a human, at what she hoped was the base of his skull.

The alien fell to the floor without another sound, and there was no sign of movement. She didn't know how to check his vital signs or determine if he was still alive, and she didn't waste time trying to find out.

Jada paused long enough to examine the wound in her arm, not wanting to leave a blood trail that would be easy to follow. The laser had cauterized the edges, so there was no blood, though it was a disgusting sight.

Before fleeing the room, she bent over long enough to try to wrest the scalpel from the back of his neck, grimacing as she realized part of the handle had gotten stuck in the light-orange spongy flesh revealed by the incision through his neck. "Gross." She wiped her hand on his slick black uniform, not wanting to think about the fact that she had alien brain matter all over her fingers.

She decided to abandon the scalpel and stood up straight, taking a moment to look through the instruments arranged on the tray, but finding nothing else that looked like the laser scalpel. She supposed she should take it out of his skull, but it wasn't much of a weapon anyway. She'd have to be in close quarters to have any use for it, and she didn't think she was going to end up catching someone else unaware again.

Before leaving the laboratory, she did pick up a metal bar out of a stack against one wall. She wasn't certain what their purpose was, but they looked like rebar used in construction. She doubted that was the function for them in this room, but when she hefted one in her hand and gave a good swing, she was satisfied it would do serious damage to any alien she actually managed to hit with it. It was still a feeble weapon, especially since they probably had something like laser rifles, but it would have to do. The only other option was to stay in the room and hide, which would be useless, because someone would eventually come check on the alien assigned to experiment on her.

At the door, she found a matching button to the one that had been on the exterior and pressed it. She held her breath as the door opened, relieved that it had done so, while also frightened of what she was going to find on the other side. She hated feeling so helpless and fearful, but there was certainly an element of adrenaline to the whole ordeal that made her feel alive.

She could almost understand extreme sports, but still didn't get how people could enjoy a career as a spy or something along those lines. That was how she felt at the moment, creeping down the corridor as she waited to run into the next alien. Unfortunately, she was no James Bond. Hell, she wasn't even a Bond Girl, and she was in way over her head.

When she got to the end of the corridor, she took a right, because they had taken a left before. She slipped down the hallway when she heard footsteps coming from the other side of the corridor. Panicked, she looked around for somewhere to hide and darted to the closest door. She could only hope it was someplace safe, rather than leading her into Dr. Ha's personal quarters, or an equally awful location.

Fortunately, the door opened when she pressed the button, and she was able to slip across the threshold and out of the way before it closed, crouching down against the wall as she waited for them to pass. She couldn't actually hear activity in the hallway, which hindered her ability to determine when it was safe to leave the darkened room.

Finally, after several seconds, she started to rise and reach for the button to allow her to exit. A second later, arms enfolded her, and a hand clamped over her mouth, trapping the scream that came automatically to her lips. Her pipe clattered to the floor with a clanking sound.

"Hush, Jada."

She froze in shock as the familiar voice whispered in her ear, turning in his arms a moment later when he loosened his hold and throwing herself into Ryland's embrace. She clung tightly to him, and after a moment, she realized he was holding her just as securely. Tears she hadn't been aware of wanting to cry suddenly filled her eyes. Jada sniffed and blinked them back while she looked up at him in the dimly lit room. The only illumination came from a device in his hand. "I was scared I'd never see you again."

His expression betrayed his concern, and his normally golden complexion was more of a pasty yellow. "What are you doing here? I told you not to come."

She stepped back from him as irritation swelled. Her hands found purchase on her hips as she glared up at her alien lover. "They came to my apartment and took me. And just what are you doing here? Your note said you were just going to poke around the outside for now and wait until dark to slip inside."

He looked sheepish. "I saw an opportunity to sneak inside, so I seized it. I've been slowly exploring the facility, and both my hearts nearly exploded when I saw you slip into this room. You aren't supposed to be here." He sounded aggravated, but she knew it wasn't at her. "You were supposed to be safe."

She bit her lip before allowing her hands to fall back to her sides and taking a step toward him again. She rested her head on his chest and one hand on his shoulder. "You're supposed to be safe too. What are we going to do?"

His arms came around her again, still holding her tightly, but perhaps without the same hint of desperation as before. "I managed to contact my supervisor, and he's agreed to send a team to apprehend Ha and his cohorts."

She shuddered in his arms. "How long will that take? Aren't you like a gazillion light-years away from here?"

"I'm in the same room, Jada," he said with perfect logic, though his lips twitched to suggest he was teasing her. "However, Dazonia Major is quite a far journey from here. Fortunately, it doesn't take long to fold."

She shook her head. "Fold? What are you folding? I don't understand."

"Essentially, we're folding space to shorten the distance between one point and another point. Reinforcements will be here within the hour."

Relief filled her, and she sagged against him. "So we just have to stay hidden until then?"

He stiffened, and there was a significant pause before his arm spasmed around her in a tight hug for a moment. After that, he took a step back, looking slightly ill. "We could do that, but I have a better idea. I don't wish to endanger you, but nor can I leave you here hiding alone. Neither option is safe."

She shook her head. "What options? Tell me what they are, and I'll decide what to do for myself."

Ryland inclined his head. "We can stay here and hide together, moving if necessary, or we can return to the holding area to free your friends and heal as many of them as time allows."

"The second idea, of course." She hesitated, tipping her head to the side as she considered. "Why do you want to heal them right this minute? I'm not ungrateful at all, but it seems like bad timing."

Ryland shrugged. "Two reasons, I suppose. The first is, healthy patients might have a greater chance of being able to escape than women who are bedbound or wheelchair-bound. The second is complicated."

She nodded to encourage him to continue.

"I'm not entirely confident my government will release the treatment for Kaiser's Syndrome without demanding the women cooperate with breeding experiments in return. I'd like to heal as many as possible before I lose the opportunity, and perhaps your scientists will find a way to reverse engineer our technology if my home world is being difficult."

She blinked at him. "But if you take away their negotiating tool, it could mean your species will go extinct."

He hesitated, his expression dark and clearly revealing his confliction. "Yes, but do we deserve to persevere and endure at the expense of your species, and the human women's right to choose whether or not to help us? That's a question I've wrestled with, and my conclusion is this has to be a consensual arrangement between Dazon men and human women, or it's completely unethical."

She nodded her satisfaction, agreeing completely with his conclusion, but still touched that he could think about it in such a way when his race's existence was at stake. "Let's go free my friends."

Chapter Five

WHEN THEY SLIPPED INTO the corridor, it was empty, and they cleared three hallways before they ran across an alien. At first, the assistant paid them little attention, probably having seen Earth women moving around the corridors before, but he stiffened as he started to pass them. He turned face Ryland, hand clamped over his upper arm. "Who are you, and what is your authorization to be in this area?"

Ryland gave him an impassive expression. "I'm Inquisitor Breese, and my authorization comes from Dazonia Major." Before the other alien could respond or react, the device in Ryland's hand crackled with green sparks, and the alien's body jolted at the impact. He convulsed and slumped to the floor a second later, either unconscious or dead.

"You tased him."

Ryland look down at her, a question in his eyes. "I did what?"

She waved a hand, deciding not to initiate a discussion on human weapons at the moment. "Never mind. Is he dead?"

Ryland nodded. "I couldn't take chances, so the pulser is discharging at maximum capacity." He took a moment to lift the body over his shoulder and nodded for her to open the nearest door. She did so cautiously, relieved to see it was another darkened room. It could be minutes or hours before someone entered, but it appeared to be empty at the moment at least. Ryland dropped the body inside, closing the door behind him with his elbow, before taking her hand and leading her down the corridor again.

That was the only alien they ran across on their trek to the area he had called the holding area, and when he opened the door to take her inside, she realized why he'd called it that.

It had an open floor plan, and the area was crammed with hospital beds. She didn't have time for an exact count, but certainly at least four hundred, and probably more. There was no doubt a bed in this facility for every woman Dr. Ha's group had kidnapped. Somewhere in the collection, there was probably a bed for her too.

"Oh, no," called out a familiar voice, thick with tears. "Not you too, Jada."

Her gaze unerringly sought the source of the voice, and tears filled her eyes when she saw her friend Jessminda a dozen beds away. She rushed to her friend, dropping down onto the bed to hug her as Ryland stood behind her.

Jess glared up at him, tightening her arms around Jada in a protective fashion. "You stay away from her."

Jada patted her shoulder and wriggled free of the tight hug, since it was currently reducing her ability to inflate her lungs. "No, it's okay, Jess. This is Ryland, and he's here to help rescue and heal you guys." She didn't bother to explain that it wasn't completely healing, but rather a process of restoring optimal homeostasis. The scientific talk and explanation could wait until later.

She looked down at her friend, who wasn't confined to the bed with straps, other than one across her waist. She touched it and arched a brow. "Have they labeled you a flight risk?"

Jess chuckled darkly. "They got sick of me pulling myself out of bed and trying to crawl across the floor."

"Never give up, right?" She grinned at her friend before turning her head to look up at Ryland. "Can you heal Jess now?"

He nodded, pulling out the same device she recognized from when he had injected her with the nanobots. "I have approximately twenty units in here, Jada, so I can't heal everyone. I wish I could."

She nodded her understanding, suddenly aware of the eyes on them, and hating the fact they couldn't help everyone or save everyone that day.

When Ryland brought the device closer to Jess, her friend shook her head, straight brown hair flying everywhere. "Get that away from me, alien boy."

"It's okay, Jess. He gave me the same thing, and I was up walking around a few minutes later."

Jess turned distrusting eyes on her, which hurt. "How am I supposed to believe that? How do I even know you're you? These are fucking aliens, Jada."

She inclined her head. "Fair enough, but have you seen any human-like aliens walking around? Or have they all been of the Mr. Bland or the golden-skin variety?"

Jess hesitated for a moment before answering, looking almost reluctant to admit, "Just the golden boys like this one."

Jada nodded again. "They want our eggs, not us. It's the Kaiser's Syndrome that makes us genetically compatible with them. I promise you that I am your friend, and not some weird alien clone thing."

"Our eggs?"

Ryland interjected, "I found the research area, and Dr. Ha's team has harvested several hundred human eggs, but has not yet initiated the process of creating blastocysts for implantation."

Jess blinked at him before turning her attention back to Jada. There was still faint suspicion in her gaze. "I still don't know if it's you."

Jada sighed. "Do you remember when we had Mexican food six months ago? We shared half a bottle of tequila between us, and we had to wait there half the night before we were sober enough to call for a taxi to take us home?"

The mistrust in Jess's eyes faded slightly. "Yeah, okay, but tell me something only you would know."

"When you were six years old, you put slugs in Pradheep's shoes because he had pulled your hair and laughed at you in front of his friends."

Jess relaxed abruptly, looking at Ryland and holding out her arm. ""Okay, get on with it then."

Ryland didn't say anything, but his lips appeared to be twitching, and he was clearly having a difficult time holding in his amusement at her about-face and bossy tone. He injected her with the nanobots and moved on to the next woman less than ten seconds later.

Jada sat with Jess as the nanobots did their magic, watching as the women nearest them were offered the option of being treated. A surprising number of them declined, but she understood their fear. She just hoped they weren't rejecting their last chance, and she hoped Ryland wasn't the only Dazon who thought it had to be a consensual arrangement for it to work.

He was administering the seventeenth dose when the door suddenly opened, admitting Ha and a group of his assistants, who stormed into the room. They formed a semicircle between the women and the exit. A few of the women were already regaining the ability to stand, Jess included, and she climbed from the bed with moderate assistance from Jada. It would take the nanotechnology a bit of time to repair her atrophied muscles, but at least she could stand.

Jorvak looked appalled at the sight before him, and his gaze homed in on his half-brother. "Inquisitor Breese?"

The coldly impersonal way he addressed his brother boggled her mind, and she reminded herself they were aliens with a completely different culture, as Ryland had told her.

Ryland slipped the device that administered the nanotechnology back into his suit, where it seemed to disappear. She'd have to remember to ask him about their storage or pockets at some point in the future. He strode back to them, his arm going around Jada's waist in a sign of support. "Jorvak Ha, you and your assistants are under arrest for sedition. You will be extradited back to the home world, where you'll face charges of unauthorized experimentation on a non-compliant sentient race."

Ha crossed his arms over his black jumpsuit and made a production of looking around. "You've come to arrest me, Inquisitor? And who will be providing the assistance for that task? Will it be these humans, who would be no match for us even in perfect physical condition?"

His gaze moved to Jada, and he frowned at her. "Perhaps it will be the human you must have restored to health a few days ago, one who was formidable enough to kill one of my assistants, but not before her genetic material was entered into the computer. As soon as it detected the presence of nanotechnology, the system alerted me."

"Actually, it will be the armada currently orbiting Earth. I received notification from Commander Darvig approximately ten minutes ago that they have arrived, and a landing party will be here shortly."

Jorvak's haughty expression faded, replaced by one of anger and fear. "Have you fools no vision? These women hold the key to our future. All Earth women can easily be modified with a full laboratory and all Dazon technology at my disposal. It won't take much to figure out how to reprogram the genetic code so that they all carry the extra fragment.

"There are approximately four billion women on this planet, which is more than enough to revitalize not only our population, but our culture and society. Our men need wives as much as we need offspring. We've forgotten how to be a cohesive society, and women can teach us that again."

Jada shook her head, stunned at the juxtaposition of his words and his actions. "But these are the women you're planning to kidnap and force to do your bidding. How do you see them becoming some sort of harmonious integration into Dazon society and elevating your standard of living...or whatever you have in mind? The women will fight you every step of the way."

He glared at her, giving her a look that suggested he found her no more important than he would a bug pinned under a microscope. "The women will cooperate if they want to have their disease held in check. If they continue to resist, it's a simple matter to shut down the nanotechnology. If I had your nanos' exact energy signature, I could shut yours down in five minutes or less."

She glared at him with equal ferocity, taking a step forward without thinking. She almost marched right up to him and slugged him in the face, which wouldn't have been very peaceable of her, but certainly would have felt good. Instead, Ryland's hand around her wrist kept her from moving forward. "You're still talking about force and coercion. The only way this union will work is as a partnership. The women have to be ready to become your partners, and there has to be more incentive than holding their health over their head."

He shrugged. "You humans are far below us and beneath us. You should consider it an honor that we would integrate you into our society."

She rolled her eyes. "You'd integrate a strain of fungus into your society if it gave you the results you're looking for, Dr. Ha."

He inclined his head in a nod of agreement. "I see we share a similar opinion of your species then."

She turned to Ryland, who had not released his hold on her hand. "I know he's your brother, but can't you just shoot him?" She was so frustrated that the words came out staccato, and she punctuated the last one with a grunt.

"I'm afraid I don't have that authorization, Jada." He winked at her. "Now, I want you and the other women to move to the back of the room, because the commander and the rest of the team are in the facility, and they'll be breaching those doors any second. I want to minimize injury, particularly to the earthlings."

Jada nodded, understanding the need to be relegated to the back of the room and protected, though she didn't like it. She would rather stand beside him, but she knew it would be a distraction for him, rather than a helping hand. She didn't know anything about combat, and she didn't even know if Ha's people would put up a fight or if they would surrender peacefully. Either way, Ryland would be more focused, ergo safer, with her out of the immediate area.

Jess heard his words too, and she started herding the women who could walk toward the back of the room. Those who were in chairs or beds, and required assistance, took more time. She was surprised that Ha's group made no effort to stop them from moving the women, but she was glad to be able to accomplish the task quickly.

They had just moved the last of the nearest thirty women deeper into the room, closer to all the other beds, when the door opened. She had been expecting a battering ram, or the alien equivalent, to be necessary, so it was almost a letdown when the door slid open easily, and the troops entered to surround Jorvak.

He and his associates surrendered without fighting, though the doctor paused as they started to escort him from the room, looking directly at Ryland as Jada came back to him, deciding it was safe enough to approach now. "All you've done today is slow down our progress and delay the inevitable. I'm not the only one who thinks this way, Inquisitor Breese. You'll see that I have more support than you, and I'll be the hero who discovered the salvation of our race, while you'll simply be the footnote recorded as a brief impediment."

Ryland shook his head as he put his arm around Jada and pulled her nearer. "I believe you're wrong, Jorvak, but I will not willingly allow such a plan to proceed, and I won't follow any who would order such action."

The Dazon who had arrested Jorvak led him from the room, and his associates fell in line between the aliens taking them into custody. Each arrestee moved with a cocky arrogance that suggested they were certain they had nothing to fear.

Jada turned to Ryland, grasping his hand in hers. "Are they right? Will they be greeted as heroes rather than criminals?"

Ryland lifted his shoulder. "I wish I knew. I'd like to believe in the goodness of my fellow Dazon, and that they couldn't act in such a reprehensible manner, but they're also desperate, and Jorvak was right. The bonds that hold us together as a people have frazzled and split over the ensuing generations, and we're a much more selfish society than we used to be. All we can do is wait and see."

She didn't like that plan, and she clung to him tighter. "Do you have to go back?"

He froze for a moment before lifting a hand to push her kinky curls off her forehead in a tender gesture. "I'll submit a recording for my debriefing, and I can record my testimony live via our communications link. There's no pressing reason for me to return to Dazonia Major. I would like to stay here on Earth...with you...but in what capacity?"

She licked her lips and pressed her body closer to his. "I'd like to have you stay in the capacity as my lover, eventually becoming my husband—or whatever Dazons call that role—and creating children together."

His eyes darkened, and he almost purred. "So now you believe in the mating flare, my sweet human?"

She shook her head. "No, not really, but I believe in you, and how you make me feel. I want you to stay."

Ryland bent his head, bringing his lips close to hers when he said, "Forever and always, my dear mate." A second later, he sealed the promise with a kiss.

About Juno

JUNO WELLS GREW UP on Florida's Space Coast, watching the shuttles take off from Cape Canaveral. When she hit college, her childhood fantasies about space travel turned highly romantic. Now her mind reels with space adventures of fantastic alien lords in distant galaxies, and the earth women they love.

Wells' stories explore the complex, sensual relationships between inhabitants of different star systems. There are always happy endings just as there is always a new world to explore.

Have a comment? Make first contact with Juno at authorjunowells@gmail.com.

About Aurelia

AURELIA SKYE IS THE pen name Kit Tunstall uses when writing science fiction romance. It's simply a way to separate the myriad types of stories she writes so readers know what to expect with each "author."

USA Today Bestselling author Kit Tunstall lives in Idaho with her husband and two sons. She enjoys writing several genres and subgenres, but almost everything she writes has a strong romantic element. A fan of post-apocalyptic, zombie, and dystopian books, she prefers to read or view such stories from the comfort of her living room and never, ever in person.

[Website][1]

---

1. http://www.kittunstall.com

Did you love *Written In The Stars*? Then you should read *Dazon Agenda: Complete Collection*[2] by Aurelia Skye and Juno Wells!

Dazon Agenda is now available in a boxed set, featuring all six titles from the series. Each story focuses on a different couple while continuing the overarching plot. When four hundred Earth women are kidnapped, it sets in motion a course of events that change both Earth and the Dazon Empire forever. With fated mates, intrigue, mystery, battles, and handsome aliens, this series brought to you by bestselling authors Aurelia Skye and Juno Wells should have something for every fan of science fiction romance.Includes:*Written In The StarsAlien's BabiesDiplomatic AffairsMoon MadnessAcross The StarsEmperor's Assassin Bride*

---

2. https://books2read.com/u/bQZVwe

3. https://books2read.com/u/bQZVwe

Also by Aurelia Skye

Alien Baby Pact
Baby For The Brundle Commander
Baby For The Grimlock General
Baby For The Palantir Chief
Baby For The Alphan Captain

Celestial Mates
Wrong Place, Right Mate
Destined For The Drakari Warlords

Cybernetic Hearts
Mated To The Cyborg General
Claimed By The Cyborg Commander
Fated For The Cyborg Officer
Meant For The Cyborg Captain
Baby For The Cyborg General
Cybernetic Hearts: Complete Series

Harrow Bay, Volume 3

Hell Virus
Catching Hell
Surviving Hell
Bleeding Hell
Raising Hell
Sharing Hell

Howls Romance
The Jaguar Alpha's Forbidden Lover

Northstar Shifters
Northstar Heir's Scarred Mate

Olympus Station
Station Commander's Surrogate
Alien Prince's Secret Baby
Security Agent's Alien Bartender
Olympus Station Compilation

SpicyShorts
Music In My Heart
Kilted Tentacle Monster: A Search for True Love

Sweet Escapes
Hook & Wendy

Three Crones Inn
Vastly Inn-proved
Ghastly Intentions
Ghostly Inn-heritance
Three Crones Inn Compilation

True North
True North #1: Death & Deception
True North #2: Rescued & Revelations
True North #3: Fire & Ice
True North #4: Enemies & Lovers
True North #5: Truth & Tiranog
True North #6: Fight & Flight
True North #7: Love & Loss

Wounded Warriors
Relentless
Marked
Justice
Wounded Warriors Collection
Hunted

Standalone
Alien General's Rebel Consort